School Shooter

Mustafa Kulle

Acknowledgements

Special Thanks to my Editor Dr. Stephen Carver

Special Thanks to my family and friends for all their love and support.

Table of Contents

Introduction

It was on a Monday morning, May 7th 2018, when the United States of America saw the worst school shooting massacre in all its history. It is known as the 'The New Colorado High School Massacre', or 'The New Colorado Massacre'.

A young boy named Casheem Ayyub, a 17 year old teenager of Palestinian origin, went on a shooting spree that ended with him taking his own life after killing 98 people and injuring 75 others in his school.

The massacre took place in Brighton High School, in the capital Brighton in New Colorado, USA. This tragedy shook the state of New Colorado to its core. Nobody ever imagined such a thing could happen.

It all began when 2 bombs exploded in the cafeteria of Brighton High School, during a recess. After the explosions, people ran out of the building in panic, meeting their deaths where the gunman awaited outside.

Casheem Ayyub shot as many as he could with his Uzi sub-machine guns. Bearing a black leather trench coat, he carried with him an entire arsenal of weapons including a pair of baretta pistols, a revolver, a pair of uzis, a 12-gauge pump action sawed-off shotgun, an M16 assault rifle, and even hand grenades. He had with him a black leather duffle bag full of rounds of ammunition which was more than enough to kill everyone in the entire school twice. Most of these weapons were bought in the local Wal-Mart, and it is still being investigated as to how he obtained some of the other weapons, such as the hand grenades.

What concerns me is that a witness, Laurence Samson, bumped into Casheem during the rampage, but the gunman spared his life. I find it very odd that a murdering maniac hell-bent on killing people without any discrimination can suddenly become so choosy. Based on what I've seen on the footage of some surveillance cameras, there was a brief dialog between them before Casheem let the witness go. He looked as though he was begging for his life, perhaps as a spontaneous response, Casheem decided not to kill this one. I must find out why. I shall take him in for questioning, and see what else I can find out from him.

One of his intended targets was Sandy Walker who was hiding in the girls' locker room when Casheem kicked the door open and threw in a hand grenade. He took a few steps back from the door and then after the explosion he took out a pair of Uzis from inside his trench coat. When a few of the girls tried to escape, he fired rounds of bullets. None of them survived. He kicked the corpses to roll over so he could identify them. Seeing that none them was his intended target, he went into the locker room and killed all the girls who were hiding. When he killed Sandy Walker, he shot her in the face and all over her body to guarantee her death.

As he walked down the hallway towards the sports hall where most of the "Jocks" hung around, he confronted the gang of big boys who apparently bullied him. One of them was Rueben Bradford, the leader of the pack. Casheem first shot Rueben's comrades so he can watch them die in front of him. He kept shooting until he was out of ammunition. He threw the Uzis away and produced a 12-Gauge Pump-Action Shotgun out from his trench coat. Reuben tried to run but Casheem shot him in the legs, preventing his escape. As Rueben helplessly crawled on the floor, Casheem slowly approached him and when he got to him, he stamped on one of his legs, giving Rueben severe agony. He then rolled him over with his foot so that Rueben was laying on his back. He could be seen shaking his head, most likely begging for mercy. Then Casheem stood over his chest, aimed his shotgun at the bully's face and blew his head off at point blank range. He too had to have a closed casket for his funeral.

Casheem then headed for the stairs where more students tried to escape to the ground floor. He shot them all, one by one with his shotgun. The force of the guns was so powerful they fell a few paces back. They all died instantly as he aimed for their chests.

Unable to escape, many of the students ran the other way to hide in the classrooms. Casheem ascended the stairs, when he couldn't open their doors, he shot through them with his guns. Once he injured the students behind the doors, he would kick the doors open and blast rounds of ammunition until everyone in the room died.

Eventually the police arrived and surrounded the building. When the police gave Casheem an ultimatum to stop, come out of the building and give himself up, he ignored them and the police opened fire. As the surveillance cameras show, Casheem took off his trench coat, threw it on the floor, put down the duffle bag and took out an M16 assault rifle. He began to shoot at the police force as they fired through the windows. As Casheem fired through one of the windows, taking cover, the police wounded him by shooting his shoulder. At that moment, a SWAT team was sent to enter the building. But it was too late. Casheem managed to crawl to his duffle bag, rummaged through and took out of his revolver. He placed it in his mouth and pulled the trigger. He was dead by the time the SWAT team reached him, they declared the massacre over and the pronounced the gunman dead. Afterwards, before the paramedics arrived, the SWAT team took pleasure in kicking Casheem's body, and spitting on him, unaware they were being recorded on camera. Their actions are being questioned.

This later became known as the Brighton High School Massacre for its masses of casualties. Hundreds more were wounded. Many more were too scared to talk about it afterwards; while others didn't want to go there again, hoping to change school. Some even went as far as to move out of the city.

My name is Billy Marksman, Inspector of the Brighton Police Department, and I am going to interview the people who knew the gunman who committed the worst school shooting America has ever seen.

It was no surprise to me that soon after the shooting, the television screens were filled with footage taken from the surveillance cameras and mobile phones, eye-witness accounts, debating "experts" and every person in the neighborhood voicing their opinions on the shooting. Many demanded more gun laws, installing metal-detectors in schools, introducing ID cards for students and authorized staff only etc. Some went as far as to suggest placing 'The Ten Commandments' in every classroom across America, compulsory church attendance, banning certain genres of music (in this case rock and heavy metal), video games and movies and even providing training for teachers to shoot any school shooter etc.

I've been hearing all this stuff on the radio, seeing it on TV and reading it in the newspapers, and on the internet. But I've had enough; it seems to me that nobody really knows anything about as to how and why this happened.

Furthermore there was a backlash against Palestinians and Muslims by the media, resulting in many who were in this demographic being stigmatized. This sickens me because I strongly believe the media has got this all wrong; there are many Palestinians and Muslims in America who wake up every day to go to work, to school, and they do not spontaneously decide to commit mass shootings.

I am a devout Catholic, and I must stress even my fellow brethren are capable of such acts of cruelty. This is about something deep, something more sinister, which I dread to find out. I feel that there is a bigger picture behind all this; everybody is ignoring the elephant in the room instead of accepting the reality of what really turned a young school boy into a mass-murdering gunman.

Before I begin though, I've done some reading into this boys' background. It doesn't paint a pretty picture.

Casheem Ayyub A.K.A. Cash was a 17 year old Palestinian boy who had problems with his school. I read stories about how he was bullied and his transformation from being a happy enthusiastic kid to becoming a quiet, isolated mystery.

As I read more about this boy, I learned that after he finished his homework he played video games and listened to rock music in his spare time. He likes retro bands like "Metallica", "Sepultura", "Nirvana" and "Pearl Jam", a range of thrash metal and grunge. His favourite band is "The Truckers", currently a popular punk rock band.

Soon after the shooting, there have been campaigns to ban video games and violent movies. Ironically, the campaigners thought Casheem watched "Natural Born Killers", a film watched by the Columbine High School shooters. But there is no evidence to support the claim that Casheem ever saw that movie. His favorite movie was "Grease 2". I wonder if the press knows of this, if so, then why do they choose to ignore it? Perhaps it doesn't suit their "let's vilify the violent genre" agenda.

I read the shooter's diaries and suicide notes, and took the time to analyze his exercise books as they show the clear signs of mental breakdown.

They start off all happy, joyful, and hopeful. He drew pictures of motorbikes, riders, and he even sketched a picture of himself riding a motorbike with a girl sitting behind him. There was a name with an arrow pointing to the girl. Later, the name was scribbled off. After careful analysis, the girl's name turned out to be 'Sandy'. A lover, perhaps? He drew pictures of guitars and drew the name of the band "The Truckers" in several places. Casheem seems to be quite a fan of heavy metal music. Contrary to what the media is saying, there is no mention of

Marilyn Manson in any of his books; nor are there any of his albums in Casheem's room. Once again, they got the wrong artist to demonize.

In reference to his diary, the year begins with his writing all enthusiastic, full of joy and much to look forward to in life. It all seems completely innocent. He drew some funny doodles, and wrote some romantic poetry. However, all this, transitions into something frightening. He draws pictures of guns, bombs, people being killed, nooses, stick figures being mutilated, and suicidal images. He even drew some swastikas and spirals that he would later graffiti everywhere. What I found was a written record of a downward spiral going from hurt and sadness to expressions of anger and hate.

But some things don't add up, which is why I must question some of the people he knew, and those who knew him.

Laurence (Larry) Samson – The Key Witness

Aged 17, according to footage from a surveillance camera, he was seen running down a hallway until he encountered the gunman, who doesn't shoot him, and instead lets him escape. It's quite bizarre how Casheem Ayyub almost had an unprejudiced shooting spree until that moment. I shall interview him first as he seems keen to talk.

BM:
I'd like you to start from the beginning Mr. Samson, when did you first see Casheem before the shooting?

LS:
Around when the school year started.

BM:
Were you friends with him?

LS:
No.

BM:
Were you in the same class?

LS:
No.

BM:

It's very odd that you encounter him during the massacre, and he doesn't kill you. Why?

LS:

I don't know. It was crazy. I was trying to find my way out of the hallway. I was running, I turn a corner and there he was. Standing there, he was wearing a trench coat, he had a shotgun in his hand! I was frightened, in my panic I slipped and I fell to the floor. And that's when he turned to look at me, he aimed the shotgun right at my face. He looked angry at first, but when he realized it was me, he put it down and looked away, looking very sad.

BM:

And then what happened?

LS:

He said "You're a good guy, Larry. Get out of here!" So I got up and ran the other way. I couldn't understand why at the time because the whole thing was a nightmare.

BM:

Was there any particular reason why he spared your life?

LS:

I don't know, we only met and spoke once.

BM:

When was this? What happened?

LS:

I can't remember when exactly, a few weeks before the shooting. One time I saw Thomas Grey trip Cash over,

I helped him up. But when I carried on going to class, I heard a big laughter in the hallway. Thomas threw a baseball at Cash's face, I felt sorry for the guy. His face was bleeding, it looked nasty. So when he carried on walking, I gave him a tissue. I asked him if he was okay, and he said he was fine.

BM:

What made you want to help Casheem?

LS:

Anybody would give somebody a hand if they were in trouble.

BM:

Of course, that's one reason why he spared you. It seems you were the only person who was ever nice to him.

LS:

I guess so. Like I said, I felt sorry for the guy.

BM:

Who's Thomas Grey?

LS:

Huh? Some jock, he's one of Rueben's gang members.

BM:

Rueben who?

LS:

Rueben Bradford. Those guys are bastards. They make everyone's life a misery, they push everyone around touching girls, you know, bullies. The worst thing is, the teachers do nothing and they get away with it.

BM:

Do you know of anything else concerning a connection between Casheem and this gang?

LS:

Oh yeah. Everybody was talking about them. Rueben and his thugs would constantly beat him up, push him around, calling him names and everything.

BM:

Did you see this bullying?

LS:

Yeah. I saw this one other incident when Phillip Dawson took Cash's phone and smashed it on the floor.

BM:

Phillip Dawson?

LS:

Yeah. He's another one of Rueben's friends. He tried to take my Blackberry, but I outran him. He couldn't catch me. The guy's a real slimeball.

BM:

What else did you see?

LS:

I saw Amanda talking to Thomas Grey during recess. It was weird.

BM:

What was unusual about that?

LS:

The girls are scared of them because those guys are always touching them up, sexually harassing them, and everything.

BM:

Do you know who this girl was?

LS:

Yeah. Amanda Walker. She's one of Sandy's friends.

BM:

What do they have to do with each other?

LS:

I don't know.

BM:

What else did you see?

LS:

At one time I saw Jacob talking to Rueben.

BM:

Jacob?

LS:

Jacob Amram, some Jewish kid. His real name is Yakov, but he prefers to be called Jacob.

BM:

What do you know about him?

LS:

He wanted to exchange my Blackberry for his old Nokia phone. I told him to go screw himself. He's always looking for business. You know, ripping people off.

BM:

What does he have to do with Casheem?

LS:

I thought they were friends until I saw him talking to Rueben. Something didn't feel right. Also, I saw him ask out Sandy on Valentine's Day and she turned him down.

BM:

When was the last time you saw Casheem?

LS:

It was when he got kicked out of 'Yeehah! Burgers', I was going in for my shift when I heard some commotion between him and the boss.

BM:

You work there was well? What happened?

LS:

Yeah, I heard Mick yell at Cash. The next thing I saw was Cash walking out looking sad and then cry.

BM:

Any idea what it was about?

LS:

This was because some drunk black guy collided with a parked car and it turned out it belonged to the boss. Mick ran out yelling, he tried to turn the engine on to chase the guy, but it wouldn't start. So he got out looking all pissed off. You do not want to get in his way when he's mad. Afterwards I heard some noises, and that's when I heard him shout at Cash. He yelled "You're fired!"

BM:

When was this?

LS:

One week before the shooting happened.

BM:

Did you see Casheem before that?

LS:

No.

BM:

But if you worked together in the same place, then you must have known more about him.

LS:

I don't. I work at night, he worked in the hours after school. I would take over after he left.

BM:

Was there anything else you saw that seemed out of the ordinary?

LS:

Yeah, one day I saw Cash go to the Principal's office and he yelled at him. He came out looking more sad. Next, on the same day, I saw a cheerleader walk in, she was crying. And then she came out crying, she was still crying, harder than before.

BM:

Casheem, and a cheerleader? Do you know of a connection between the two?

LS:

I don't know, but I knew something was wrong. All I know is this cheerleader is one of Sandy's friends. And truth be told, the Principal is not a likable guy. He's really cold, more like a Corporate Executive than a Principal. He sits in that comfortable office all day, doing nothing. That old fart, he's an asshole.

BM:

Given everything you've told me; do you think all this contributed to Casheem wanting to take some sort of revenge?

LS:

Oh yeah, definitely. I have no doubts about that.

Mick Harrison, Casheem's Former Employer, Owner of 'Yeehah! Burgers'

Aged 47, he has a history of behavior problems caused by his drinking habits. He's been attending therapy sessions, but records show that he hasn't been turning up lately and he's been drinking more. Perhaps it's his addiction, or maybe his way with people given how he treated Casheem last. But I must obtain more information from this man.

BM:
How did you come to know Casheem?

MH:
Well, he came to my diner and he asked me for a job and I said "Yeah".

BM:
When was this?

MH:
Pff... I dunno. Early October I think.

BM:
He was a good employee?

MH:

Yer God damn right. He knew how to flip burgers, fry potatoes and keep the place spotless.

BM:

What was he like when he first started?

MH:

He was quite a chatterbox. He was a happy kid. He was good with the customers and a damn good cook. Not like the kids today who just come home and say "Mom, what's for dinner?" Nope. That ain't Cash.

BM:

Did you notice anything strange about him?

MH:

When he first started, he was keen, determined like he really wanted to earn money. He worked overtime too. One day he was really excited, the next he looked awfully sad.

BM:

When was this change?

MH:

Some time after February 14th.

BM:

You didn't suspect anything?

MH:

Boys like him are always gloomy during Valentine's Day and after, I presume there was some girl involved and it didn't go very well. I thought he'd get over it.

BM:
Did he?

MH:
I don't think so. Over time he got quieter and quieter. I don't know why. He just kept to himself. He spoke less. That didn't bother me. He was doing a good job.

BM:
Did you have any idea that something was bothering him outside work?

MH:
No, but I didn't care. His problems are his problems, not mine.

BM:
When was the last time you saw him?

MH:
Uhh... it was a week before the shooting.

BM:
What happened? Did he not show up for work before that?

MH:
No. What's that got to do with this?

BM:
I need to know the circumstances which triggered the

shooting.

MH:

Well that's got nothing to do with me.

BM:

I'm not blaming you entirely however there is a correlation.

MH:

Correlation? That massacre and my business are unrelated! Just because that kid happened to be my former employee that don't make me responsible for his actions. I don't care what happened in that school, oh well, too bad. Life goes on.

BM:

Then why are you being so defensive?

MH:

It's because you're making me feel uncomfortable with all the damn questions you're askin'! Making it out like it's my fault.

BM:

What happened on the day you saw him last?

MH:

I was havin' a bad day. The suppliers weren't answering my calls and we had some bad customers.

BM:

Where does Casheem come into this?

MH:

Some nigger driver smashed into my car in the parking lot and got away before I could catch him. God damn son-of-a-bitch, I still haven't got my car fixed yet.

BM:

And then?

MH:

So I marched back into the kitchen. I was so furious I didn't see Cash and accidentally knocked him over. He was in my way and I yelled at him "You're fired!" When he protested, I yelled some more and told him to never come back.

BM:

Why did you do that?

MH:

I don't know. Like I said, I was having a bad day and he just happened to be there. I lost my temper and I took it out on him.

BM:

You do indeed have issues involving your temper, don't you?

MH:

Hey, you don't know anything about me.

BM:

I sure do. Care to explain your alcohol addiction?

MH:

What?! How the hell d'ya… to hell with you! So what?! I have to have something to get me through. Nothing beats a bottle of Jack Daniel's when your wife's giving you hell. "Mick, do this". "Mick, do that". I hate that shit.

BM:

Yes, and I know you harm those around you when you're mad, especially when you're drunk.

MH:

Yeah, well, what's done is done.

BM:

How did you feel after you fired Casheem?

MH:

It felt good at the time, stress relief, you know. But then I felt rotten about it. I was going to give him his job back, with two week's pay, but I never got round to makin' that phone call.

BM:

Do you feel responsible for what happened afterwards?

MH:

Hell no! I ain't the one who sold him the guns.

Amanda Walker, Sandy Baker's Friend

Aged 17, she was one of Sandy Baker's friends who is also a fellow cheerleader. I'm not sure how she's connected to Casheem exactly, but I am certain she has more information that may help piece together what happened at Brighton High.

BM:
Were you in the same class as Casheem?

AW:
Yeah.

BM:
What was Casheem like when he first started?

AW:
He was kind of weird.

BM:
In what way?

AW:
I don't know. He was just weird.

BM:

How did he behave towards you?

AW:

Ummm...well, he would say "Hey. How are you?" and I just look the other way. He was making me feel awkward. Everybody was laughing at him, and I didn't want them to laugh at me so I told him to "Get lost".

BM:

That's no way to treat others. Is it?

AW:

No, I guess not.

BM:

Why is it now that you doubt such behavior?

AW:

I don't know. It's just normal. Look, I didn't know what was going to happen next.

BM:

So it all requires a mass shooting to change your behavior?

AW:

Hey, that's not fair, you take that back!

BM:

I certainly will not. As you and everybody else in the school gave him the same treatment. You made him an outcast. He was only trying to be nice, make friends with you. Is that not what you do in school?

AW:

I guess.

BM:

What happened to Casheem on Valentine's Day?

AW:

Cash gave Sandy a rose and we laughed at him.

BM:

Why?

AW:

Because it was funny. I mean the guy's a total loser and he didn't stand a chance. A geek like him and a cheerleader like her? Forget it. Anyway, she took the rose and then threw it in the trash when he wasn't looking.

BM:

I see. Tell me something, do you like "The Truckers"? Good band, are they?

AW:

Well, they're not exactly my kind of music.

BM:

So why did you go to their concert with Sandy?

AW:

I don't know, she had two tickets to go to a gig and she invited me, so I thought "Why not?"

BM:

What if I told you that one of those tickets wasn't for you?

AW:

Huh?

BM:

What if that ticket was meant for someone else? Did you know about that?

AW:

No. Was it?

BM:

Yes. Casheem bought those tickets.

AW:

Really? How did she get hold of them?

BM:

She offered to look after them until then. When that night came, he was knocking on her door and her father chased him away with death threats. She had already gone out, with you.

AW:

Oh...

BM:

You knew, didn't you?

AW:

Not until afterwards. It was funny. We had fun.

BM:

He worked hard for those tickets, don't you feel any shame, or remorse?

AW:

Well, yeah, kind of. How do you know about all this?

BM:

He kept a diary. He also mentioned in it the day after the gig, you and your friends laughed in his face, calling him a 'loser'. Did you?

AW:

No.

BM:

Sure you didn't. It's bad enough you ruined his date only to mock him afterwards. Has it not crossed your m i n d to apologize to Casheem?

AW:

No, we don't do things like that.

BM:

Not even to pay back the ticket that he paid for, that you used?

AW:

No. Besides, I thought he'd get over it.

BM:

Were you not aware of how deeply hurt he was?

AW:

No. He's a geek. Well, he was. You're not supposed to care about things like that.

BM:

Before the shooting, you were seen talking to Thomas Grey, want to tell me what that was all about?

AW:

Uuh, nothing.

BM:

Really? You, Sandy, and all the other girls don't like that sort, do you? So why would you talk to one of them?

AW:

It was nothing. Really. I was just flirting with him, that's all. You know, to sweeten things up between us.

BM:

Is that so? Despite all this, do you feel responsible for what happened afterwards?

AW:

No. I wasn't the one who turned down his offer. Sandy was my best friend, at least I'm glad he didn't ask me for a date. I would have been humiliated and he would have targeted me instead.

Phillip Dawson, Rueben's Friend

Aged 18, according to Lawrence's statement, he was one of the bullies who routinely tormented Casheem, this will be interesting. I wonder how much he will confess.

BM:

Tell me Mr. Dawson, why do you go to school?

PD:

Uh, to learn things, to get smart, so you can get a job.

BM:

Well you don't have good track record, the highest grade you ever got was a 'C+'.

PD:

Hey, fuck you, man!

BM:

So come on, tell me, why do you really go to school?

PD:

It's the sports. Ya know. Football is the best! It's a man's game. If you're no good at it, then you're a faggot, a pussy.

BM:

Is that why you and Rueben were picking on Casheem?

PD:

Yeah, he was a total loser. He couldn't challenge anybody. It got worse when the coach put him on our team in class, he totally sucked. He put him in our team on purpose for his own amusement.

BM:

But he was a good pupil, hard working, well-behaved, an 'A' student. What's not to like about that?

PD:

Ew, man! Nah, that's pathetic. It's just not cool.

BM:

But picking fights with someone who's unable to defend himself is?

PD:

Look, man, if you don't do these things, people will walk all over you. So we have to get with the program and Cash just wasn't part of it. It's all about fear and respect.

BM:

Rueben didn't have much respect for you either, he threatened you a few times, didn't he?

PD:

Shut up! He would have killed me if I didn't do what he said.

BM:

So you'd tag along with a bully just to make you feel strong?

PD:

No. I just didn't want to be like Cash. You can't go it alone. It made things easier that way.

BM:

You mean you were scared of him.

PD:

What?! Fuck you!

BM:

Did you not think Casheem was more scared? Did you not think of protecting him, or being his friend? You're a lot stronger than him.

PD:

No because Rueben would have given me the same treatment.

BM:

I thought so. What did you do to Casheem?

PD:

All kinds of things, the classic stuff, you know. The pushing, the shoving, tripping him over, calling him names, humiliating him, it was fun.

BM:

Is that all?

PD:

Yeah.

BM:

Are you sure? Won't you tell me what you guys did to him back in March?

PD:

Nah. I don't remember.

BM:

An incident took place in the locker room and you were involved.

PD:

No I wasn't.

BM:

How can you remember so well now?

PD:

Well... uh... the locker room is part of our routine. Nothing out of the ordinary there.

BM:

Come on, you've contradicted yourself already. First you say you don't remember only to tell me you had nothing to do with an incident. Which is it?

PD:

No. Nothing happened.

BM:

Not even an incident involving Casheem?

PD:

No.

BM:

Okay, let's have a look at your attendance record. Throughout March, 2018, you never missed a single sports class which means you were in the locker rooms every time. In other words, whatever took place in the locker rooms in that time period you were present.

Upon further investigation, prior to the shootings, traces of blood were found on the shower floor. That blood belonged to Casheem.

And lastly, Casheem mentions you in his diary... saying you kicked him.

Are you still going to tell me "nothing out of the ordinary" happened last March?

PD:

But... I didn't do anything. I swear.

BM:

Let's hear your side of the story then.

PD:

Alright. We just finished sports class and we were bored. So we took his bag and tossed it around. He tried to get it back but then Rueben held it under a shower and it made his books all wet. We were all laughing and he was sad. Then he got mad and threw the first slap at him but he missed.

BM:

And then?

PD:

Rueben punched him the face and Cash fell on the floor in a second. It was a one-hit knockout! And then we all gathered around him and we kicked him until he was bleeding.

BM:

So you left him there on the wet shower floor bleeding, and you didn't think to assist him at all?

PD:

No.

BM:

Why?

PD:

What do you mean "Why"?

BM:

Why did you not help him?

PD:

I don't know.

BM:

Well, now that we've refreshed your memory on one incident, do you want to tell me about the other incident?

PD:

Which one?

BM:

The time you filmed the drowning in the toilet?

PD:

Oh...uh... I had nothing to do with that.

BM:

Sure, after all, it was uploaded to the internet from Rueben's phone. But he didn't film it because he was the one holding Casheem's head down the toilet. The rest of you gathered around laughing like wild hyenas. One of you filmed it. You weren't visible in the footage per se but sure enough your voice and your laughter could be heard in close proximity to the recording phone. When we examined the origin of the footage on Rueben's phone, we traced it back to your phone.

PD:

Look, he just told me to film it, ok! I didn't know he was going to put it on the internet! Geez... I mean, it was funny. But what was I supposed to do? How was I supposed to know what he was going to do?

BM:

Is that all you have to say about that? It was viewed all over the world. People are still commenting on it as we speak. Can you imagine how embarrassing that must have been for him? Did you find it funny afterwards?

PD:

No, not really. It went stale after three flushes, we didn't know it was gonna go this far.

BM:

What about you? You took things further didn't you?

PD:

What do you mean?

BM:

On top of kicking him, then filming his torment, according to his diary you damaged his property. Is this true?

PD:

Er... what property?

BM:

We have acquired surveillance camera footage of the very incident. You gonna tell me that wasn't you?

PD:

Um... Okay, fine! I didn't like him either. His face. His high grades. Those heavy metal t-shirts. I mean, he was a freak, I had to show the world what I was made of. He had a Samsung smartphone. A fucking Samsung! Why would you buy that Asian trash when you can buy American, like an Apple? We all have iPhones and he was carrying around an Asian piece of crap. It's totally un-American. Someone had to teach him a lesson.

BM:

So, to do that you took his phone and smashed it on the floor?

PD:

Yeah, it felt good. He tried to wrestle me afterwards but I lifted him up and put him in a trash can. He was as light a feather. After that, I kicked the trash can so he rolled with it. It was quite a show, everyone saw it and they laughed. It was funny.

BM:

Very sensitive of you. How do you feel about it now?

PD:

You know, I'm not so sure. It's crazy. You never expect anybody like that to pick up a gun and start shootin' people the way he did.

BM:

No regrets?

PD:

Hey man, if I didn't do all that stuff, I wouldn't have gained half of my popularity.

BM:

So you have no responsibility for what came next?

PD:

No, it was all Rueben's fault. Everything was his idea. Not mine.

Thomas Grey, Rueben's Friend

Another 18 year old acquaintance of Rueben Bradford's, and another tormentor of Casheem's. I am keen to know what this guy has to hide, let's see what he has to say about his meeting with Amanda Walker.

BM:

Tell me what you know about Casheem.

TG:

I never liked him. I knew he was trouble the moment I saw him. He was brown.

BM:

His ethnicity and his skin colour bothered you?

TG:

Yeah, I figured he was Palestinian. That makes him an Arab, right? Besides, they're terrorists. Look what they did on 9/11.

BM:

If your crude generalization was true, there would be no American left.

TG:

Screw you, man! I hated his face. He looked so damn ugly.

BM:

Were you friends with Rueben?

TG:

Yeah, we hung around from time-to-time.

BM:

You were involved in bullying Casheem too?

TG:

Yeah.

BM:

But he never bothered you, so why would you mistreat him?

TG:

He was a walking comedy show. One shove and he's flyin'.

BM:

Tell me something, Thomas, you were seen talking to Amanda Walker. What was the discussion about?

TG:

Amanda Walker? She told me that Casheem was harassing her, you know, being a pervert and stuff.

BM:

Really? What else did she tell you?

TG:

I don't remember exactly. She told me she wanted him to leave her alone. And he wouldn't stop following her home from school.

BM:

Amanda and Casheem lived in the same street.

TG:

Seriously? Well, she didn't tell me that. But he wouldn't leave her alone, so that was all I needed to know.

BM:

They were working on a project together in class. Did she not tell you that?

TG:

Ewww, why would she work with that terrorist?

BM:

The teacher chose them to work together.

TG:

So?

BM:

She wasn't doing her homework or any part of their project, Casheem wanted to get a good grade. It was important for him, and she pushed him away when he needed help from her.

TG:

I didn't know that. Damn, she could have told me. Oh well, nobody cares. I kind of liked her, and I wasn't going to have some sand-nigger sniffing her ass.

BM:

What did you do to him?

TG:

I let him walk past me after climbing up the stairs, I grabbed his bag and then I yanked him back so he fell down the stairs.

BM:

You could have killed him.

TG:

I don't care. After all, it was fun to watch him roll down the stairs and hit the ground the way he did. It made everyone's day.

BM:

Did you not think to talk to Casheem first?

TG:

Nah. Fight first, talk later. That's what my Dad says.

BM:

Well he's not a very bright character is he?

TG:

Shut the fuck up! You don't know nothin'!

BM:

I know he beat up your Mother and that's why he's in jail awaiting bale.

TG:

That has nothing to do with this.

BM:

I'm afraid it does, young man. It's no surprise you take up your Father's behavior and bring it to school with you to make a name for yourself.

TG:

Yeah, so?

BM:

So you used Casheem as your punch bag?

TG:

Yeah, it felt good, it takes away my frustrations.

BM:

And, what frustrations were these?

TG:

Well, Rueben was always telling me what to do and it made me mad.

BM:

So your inability to stand up for yourself against someone equal to your size made you feel weak?

TG:

No.

BM:

Then why pick on Casheem? He did nothing to you.

TG:

Everybody knows he's a loser, so I gave the school something to remember. I tripped him over when he walked past me, everybody laughed. As he made his way further down the hallway, I called his name and as he turned around, I threw a baseball at his face. He was on the floor in an instant. Hands on his face and crying. The blood on the floor was a good mark for everyone to remember and talk about. The cleaner still can't get it off the floor.

BM:

That is disgusting and unacceptable. What if the roles were reversed and he did the same to you?

TG:

He can't.

BM:

Did you know it's this sort of behavior that causes people to harm others?

TG:

You mean the mass shooting? Well, he missed me. I decided to take a day off school that day.

BM:

You don't care about anyone? Your friends or teachers who were killed?

TG:

When I turned on the TV, the only person I thought about was Amanda. I thought she was dead until she called me.

BM:

Are you going out together?

TG:

No, she doesn't want to know me anymore. I wish she were dead too.

Shirwin Mann, Principal of Brighton High School

A 57 year old former banker who was made redundant due to seniority and settled for working in this school, there's still something bothering me as to what happened to Casheem, concerning him and some girl in connection to Laurence's statement.

BM:

Were you aware of Casheem's torment?

SM:

Not until a few weeks before the shooting.

BM:

When he came to your office to report the bullying, what did you do?

SM:

I told him I'll have a word with the culprits.

BM:

Did you?

SM:

No, I just said it to put his mind at ease.

BM:

What did you tell him after he came back to you?

SM:

I told him to man up and get out of my office. However, I did call those individuals to my office. I gave them a warning that's all.

BM:

What did you say to them?

SM:

All I said to them was to leave this kid alone so he can stop bothering me. It was giving me a headache.

BM:

That didn't stop the bullying, did it?

SM:

No. He came into my office and begged me to transfer him to another class because the boys and girls were picking on him. I told him to shut up, to stop being a crybaby, and deal with it. We can't keep changing classrooms because one student won't get on with the rest of the class. If we did, that would make things... complicated.

BM:

But do you think the lack of action made things escalate?

SM:

Yes yes, but that gives you no right to go round shooting people.

BM:

Do you not feel that something could have been done to prevent the shooting from happening?

SM:

Yes, they shouldn't sell guns to kids over the counter, especially without a license.

BM:

I was referring to you, is there really nothing you could have done? After all, Casheem came to you for help and you turned him away.

SM:

Me? Not really. Maybe he could have been transferred to another school but I didn't see the point in that. He probably would have been bullied there too. Besides, these things are long and slow processes.

BM:

I would have thought a principal like you wouldn't tolerate such behavior in your school. Surely you could have disciplined those kids somehow.

SM:

The last thing I needed was the parents of these kids telling me how I should not treat their children. You know what they're like. They say things like "Don't tell me how I should discipline my child" or, "My children are angels, they wouldn't do that", and blah blah blah.

BM:

So you feared a backlash from the parents of the bullies? That's cowardly.

SM:

What would you have done?

BM:

I would have sent letters to their parents informing them of their behavior. That would be a start.

SM:

Nobody's got time for that!

BM:

There's so much you could have done, and yet you did nothing?

SM:

Listen, it's my job to keep things here under control. As you know, children will be children.

BM:

Was it really the anger of the parents that frightened you? Or was there something else?

SM:

No, nothing.

BM:

Rueben Bradford, you know his father Richard Bradford?

SM:

What about him?

BM:

Mr. Mann, I know he paid you to accept Rueben into this

school. I spoke to him. You knew he was a troubled kid, you knew he had behavior problems.

SM:

Alright, so I accepted him, so what? I needed the extra money.

BM:

For what?

SM:

That's none of your God damn business!

BM:

But Reuben found out, didn't he? He had you wrapped around his little finger and he threatened to tell everyone about your corruption.

SM:

To Hell with you! I would have been ruined if he said anything, or if I punished the boy.

BM:

There is another matter at hand. Did you know that Rueben raped a girl on the school premises?

SM:

Yes. She came to me crying. I couldn't bear to see her cry like that. She told me she was scared and begged me to call the police.

BM:

So what did you do?

SM:

I refused. I dismissed her at first. I told her never to come back without any evidence.

BM:

But there was evidence, wasn't there?

SM:

What do you mean?

BM:

Casheem mentioned her to you, didn't he?

SM:

He kept coming to my office. His face was the last thing I wanted to see. He tried to tell me something but I wasn't interested. So I told him to focus on his bullying issues and to keep his nose out of everybody's business.

BM:

But Casheem was an eye-witness.

SM:

How the hell do you know?

BM:

He mentioned it in his diary. He saw Rueben grab the girl and pull her into the Men's locker rooms. Casheem walked in and saw them in the act. He was too scared to intervene, so that's why he came to you.

SM:

And I told him to never make such statements without

proof, and then to get out of my office. That was the last time I saw him.

BM:

In short, you turned a blind eye to two victims of your school because the money of the tormentor's father was more important to you than anything else. That sums it up, don't you think?

SM:

Well, when you put it like that I... I don't know what to say.

BM:

Is there any chance you feel responsible for what happened to Casheem?

SM:

Certainly not, it's his parents' fault. They should have taught him some structure. How to be a man. How to deal with his social problems. The simple stuff everyone learns when they grow up. It's certainly not my job.

BM:

And what about the girl?

SM:

Girls like that shouldn't flirt with young men otherwise that's what they will get. Cheerleaders, the way they dress and all that sexual provocation must not be tolerated.

Jacob (Yakov) Amram, Casheem's Acquaintance

A 17 year old boy who was in Casheem's class. According to Laurence, he was a friend, but what I've read in Casheem's diary seems to show that it was a friendship that had fallen apart over some dispute which I am keen to know the details of. One thing I can't get out of my head is the fact that he was seen talking to Rueben, of all people. I would not class someone like him to be a friend of Casheem's. There must be something under the surface.

BM:
Casheem was a class mate of yours, wasn't he?

JA:
That's right.

BM:
You were good friends at one time, weren't you?

JA:
Yes.

BM:
So what happened between you?

JA:

I asked him to do my homework for me. He said he'd do it for money.

BM:

He did it well?

JA:

Yeah, he changed his handwriting to make it look like mine.

BM:

So you made a commitment to pay him for doing your homework?

JA:

Yeah, it was great. I had plenty of time to myself, and do all the things I never had time to do. It made life easier.

BM:

But that wasn't to last, was it?

JA:

I was running out of money, my Mum and Dad won't lend me anymore so I told him I couldn't pay him. He got mad at me for wasting his time. He felt betrayed but there was nothing I could do.

BM:

Yes there was. You could have just done your homework like everybody else. But let's face it, you didn't want to pay him the money. Did you?

JA:

So what?

BM:

So what happened?

JA:

I told him to give me my homework but he didn't.

BM:

Then you got detention, didn't you?

JA:

It was the most humiliating thing that ever happened to me.

BM:

Indeed it was, you, also an 'A' student, who never missed a class, always gotten straight 'A's failed to hand in your homework. And then you got detention for the first time.

JA:

Yeah, it was terrible, the whole town knew about it, they told my parents and I was grounded for a month.

BM:

But it didn't end there, did it?

JA:

What do you mean?

BM:

You were seen talking to Rueben in the cafeteria, early in

the month of March. He picked on you too at one point. What reason did you have to approach him?

JA:

I told Rueben that Cash stole my money and that he took my homework and gave it in with his name written on it. I offered to pay him $100.

BM:

Do you know what happened to Casheem after that?

JA:

No. And I don't want to know.

BM:

Oh you should, he took a real beating by Rueben and his gang alright. To add insult to injury, a teacher who overheard their dispute gave him detention, she didn't even tend to his wounds. Then she told all the other teachers that he hands in homework that doesn't belong to him. That humiliation was worst than yours.

JA:

Oh, well, I didn't mean for it to go that far. I only wanted Rueben to beat him up for me. Revenge, you know.

BM:

You paid him then?

JA:

No, I was going to give it to him after the day of the shooting. I didn't have enough money at the time, so I didn't show up to school that day. Oh well, at least he's dead, he won't be needing the $100 now.

BM:

This wasn't just about money, or your detention, was it?

JA:

It was.

BM:

Tell me your feelings about Sandy.

JA:

What about her? Why are you dragging her into this?

BM:

You did so yourself.

JA:

I don't understand.

BM:

Very well then. In reference to Casheem's diary you had an argument over her. Clearly the friendship between you two came to an end. He claims to have seen you asking out Sandy on Valentine's day, and she turned you down. But Casheem beat you to it, he asked her out before you.

JA:

I told him to stay away from her. I couldn't believe she would be interested in him. I saw her take his rose.

BM:

But she wasn't, she took it only to throw it in the trash.

JA:

But they went to the concert together, that was their date. I saw the tickets in Cash's hand.

BM:

I'm afraid that date wasn't to be. She took them from him only to go with Amanda, she stood him up. You can imagine how he felt after that, can't you?

JA:

Oh. Oh man, why did nobody tell me?

BM:

Nobody cared. He was heartbroken, with a routine of daily torment, there was really nobody for him to turn to.

JA:

I wish could take it all back.

BM:

Do you think your betrayal may have pushed him to insanity?

JA:

Maybe. Maybe not. But people get over these things.

BM:

Really? Were you over your humiliation before the massacre?

JA:

No. Not really. I was still mad about that.

BM:

See? It's not as easy as you make it out to be. You cannot forget such hurtful behavior overnight. And neither could Casheem. Have you no remorse for what you have done?

JA:

You know, now that you told me all this, I'm not so sure.

Conclusion

Having learned the details after questioning those who knew Casheem Ayyub, they cannot find it within themselves to apologize, feel guilt, or to even say "I'm sorry". At least they can't do anymore harm to Casheem. What worries me is that Casheem is not the only boy in America who is dealing with bullying, betrayals, and corruption in school. Who knows what torment they are going through right now? If nobody takes responsibility for their actions or reach out to help, I fear there will be many more school shootings like this one yet to come.

We must understand that there are millions of boys and girls who need our help, who are vulnerable, powerless, who are at our mercy. Their lives, hopes and fears intertwined with ours. We are all responsible for one another and it is our duty to help those who are less fortunate than us. This is not to sympathize with a mass murderer, certainly not, but it is to remind everybody that there are consequences for all our words and actions.

Unfortunately, the vast majority of us live our lives in some sort of auto-pilot mode, resulting in us forgetting all about our basic our human instincts, emotions, and feelings, taking such simple things for granted. We are not robots, we are people.

It seems to me that Casheem Ayyub was just an ordinary boy who had dreams, hopes and desires that have been crushed by a cold, cruel, and a heartless society. The source of all his misery was in the very place where he wanted to belong and feel a part of something of great importance. His school, Brighton High School.

Of course, there are serious problems involving guns in this country, but we must look at the bigger picture. To start, we must look in the mirror and reflect on ourselves.

The only person who showed any sign of humanity towards Casheem was Laurence. His one and only act of altruism saved his life, otherwise Casheem would have executed him too. But Casheem didn't only target the bullies who beat him, the girl who broke his heart, the principal who abandoned him, the friend who betrayed him, no, he targeted everyone in the school. Instead of everyone laughing at him, they could have stuck up for him, they could have given him a helping hand, any kind of support, or at least show sympathy. But they didn't. Casheem targeted the cold society of his school. He wanted to rid the world of the people who made his daily school life an ongoing torture.

I say with relief, the suffering is over, his deeds have been catastrophic, so we must grieve, share our guilt and prepare to change our attitudes, not just for ourselves, but for all of mankind.

There is an ancient Chinese proverb that says "Society prepares the crime, the criminal carries it out." I was hoping to prove that wrong when I took this job, because every person as an individual is responsible for their actions, but I hate to admit how true it is.

The only person who showed any sign of remorse was

Laurence Samson. But the rest aren't as sympathetic, nor want anything to do with Casheem in fear of them becoming targets of bullying too. But there is more of them than there is of the bullies, yet no-one made the effort to act against such injustice or cruelty, though it was right in front of their eyes. Sadly, nobody wants to accept the responsibility of taking action for what's right.

If we don't learn to look after one another, all humanity will perish.